Flanimals

By
Ricky Gervais

Illustrated by
Rob Steen

G. P. Putnam's Sons • New York

With many thanks to Lee

G. P. PUTNAM'S SONS
A division of Penguin Young Readers Group
Published by The Penguin Group
Penguin Group (USA) Inc., 375 Hudson Street, New York, NY 10014, U.S.A.
Penguin Group (Canada), 10 Alcorn Avenue, Toronto, Ontario, Canada M4V 3B2
(a division of Pearson Penguin Canada Inc.)
Penguin Books Ltd, 80 Strand, London WC2R 0RL, England.
Penguin Ireland, 25 St. Stephen's Green, Dublin 2, Ireland (a division of Penguin Books Ltd.)
Penguin Group (Australia), 250 Camberwell Road, Camberwell, Victoria 3124, Australia
(a division of Pearson Australia Group Pty Ltd).
Penguin Books India Pvt Ltd, 11 Community Centre, Panchsheel Park, New Delhi - 110 017, India.
Penguin Group (NZ), Cnr Airborne and Rosedale Roads, Albany, Auckland 1310, New Zealand
(a division of Pearson New Zealand Ltd).
Penguin Books (South Africa) (Pty) Ltd, 24 Sturdee Avenue, Rosebank, Johannesburg 2196, South Africa.
Penguin Books Ltd, Registered Offices: 80 Strand, London WC2R 0RL, England.

First American edition published in 2005 by G. P. Putnam's Sons,
a division of Penguin Young Readers Group, 345 Hudson Street, New York, NY 10014.
G. P. Putnam's Sons, Reg. U.S. Pat. & Tm. Off.
Published in Great Britain in 2004 by Faber and Faber Limited, London.
Manufactured in Mexico. Text set in Franz.
Library of Congress Cataloging-in-Publication Data
available upon request.
ISBN 0-399-24397-6
1 3 5 7 9 10 8 6 4 2
First Impression

There are a few things you need to
know about Flanimals. And when you do,
I'd keep them to yourself if I were you.

Contents

Chapter 1: Spotter's Guide   7

Chapter 1

Spotter's Guide

Coddleflop
(Ovarian Fliphanger)

Slurdles around absorbing stains and puddles.
Its only defense is to flip over to protect its soft top.
Unfortunately, its bottom is equally soft and is
instantly squashed if trodden on.

Plamglotis
(Taslo Epiglug)

Born without feet, it swallows its hands to walk
on to find food. Obviously, when it finds food
it can't eat it because its mouth is full.

Mernimbler

(Gruntling Flumpamorphis)

Mernimblers live on honey water and
the softer bits of clouds. They stay this way for some time,
then turn into adults when someone says, "Oh, look
at those cute little Mernimblers, I think I'll stroke one."

Adult Mernimbler
(Gruntling Flumpamorphis)

Eats everything it sees
and dies of chronic indigestion.

Grundit
(Grundoidian Yobjammer)

Staggers around half-witted and grumpy,
trying to start trouble. Its favorite hobby is using
the Puddloflaj as a form of transport, but it always
falls off, causing the bumps on its head. Luckily the
brain is too small to be affected.

Puddloflaj
(Blobbulous Boinglubber)

Cowardly wobbler that spends its days avoiding the Grundit.
The Puddloflaj looks like a useless fat blob. It actually doesn't
have an ounce of fat on it—it's water retention. In fact it's nearly
100% water, sort of like filling a balloon from a tap.
Baby Puddloflaj can be used as water bombs.

Flemping Bunt-himmler
(Guzzle Sprout Flemper)

Feeds on baby Mernimblers and replaces
them in the nest. He is exposed when they all
turn into adults and eat him.

Underblenge

(Ekino Plunge-Dermer)

Snerbulent splench-sucker that captures prey
by sticking to their faces and suffocating them—its
suckers are impossible to pry off. Unfortunately,
it can't catch anything as it can't move from
the rock it was born on.

Blunging
(Hmpahoid Strich-Hopper)

Hamble-springs around happily caring for
its young. It's not so happy when it has to watch
the adult Mernimbler rip its baby's head off.

Munty Flumple
(Lumulous Blump)

This little dough-brained chump mijlet likes everything.
It wanders around and stares at things, instantly falling
in love. It will stand staring for days until the Flanimal it is
staring at moves away. If it falls in love with a Glonk,
it is there forever.

Splunge
(Jello Snurbloid)

Quite literally a bag of nerves.
So utterly terrified of everything, it splunges at birth.
This causes both parents to do the same.

Honk
(Hagen Splurg-Klanger)

Moley squit that sleeps all day, until
for no reason it makes the loudest noise on the planet,
causing its nose to trumpet up to fifty times normal size.
It then falls to the floor, exhausted and fast asleep.

Hemel Sprot
(Podis Reversis)

Rushes across the guddle deserts on its wobble pod, only looking where it's been, never where it's going. Eventually dies by bumping into the Sprot Guzzlor.

Sprot Guzzlor
(Guzzlank Plod)

Gruntloid in build but related to the Anker.
Eats Hemel Sprots but is terrified of adult Mernimblers.

Clunge Ambler

(Humpulous Lug)

This sweaty little waddle-gimp shuffles around trying to
cuddle things. He is weird and smells, so is constantly
being beaten up and buried. He never learns his lesson and
always tries to find and cuddle the Flanimal that buried him.
The Flanimal usually buries him again.

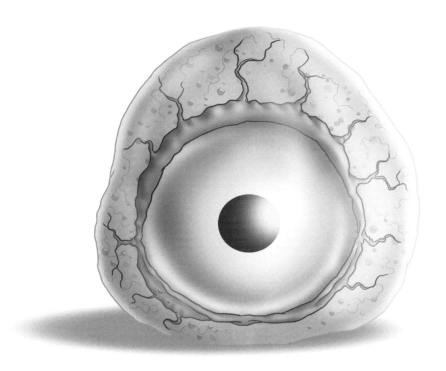

Wobboid Mump
(Lumpus Chuck-Goggler)

One of the most useless organisms in the universe.
It is basically an eye in jelly. It spends most of its time
looking around trying to find reason in its existence.
It never finds it as it is blind.

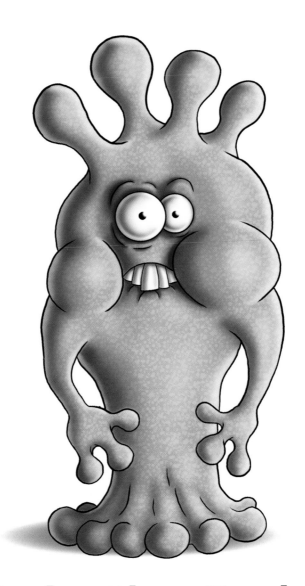

Sprine Bloat-Trunker
(Puddly Groid Bulb)

Sprouts up explosively from a fungal spume puddle
outside the sewage pump of the Sprog and Hemel Sprot
recycling plant. It immediately joins the queue
to be recycled.

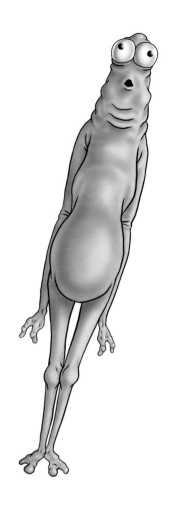

Print

(Addle-Sprungnurdler)

Small sprooding creature that
dives around, sometimes off tall rocks,
but always manages to land on its head.
They usually die from landing badly in
strong wind and spraining their ankle.

Gum Spudlet
(Dentoid Mashler)

Grundit food.
It's not happy about this but it can't bite back.

Sprog
(Scousious Angroid)

Honionoidly angry about its breath, the Sprog bounces and squeaks around until it is chewed up and spat out by a Grundit.

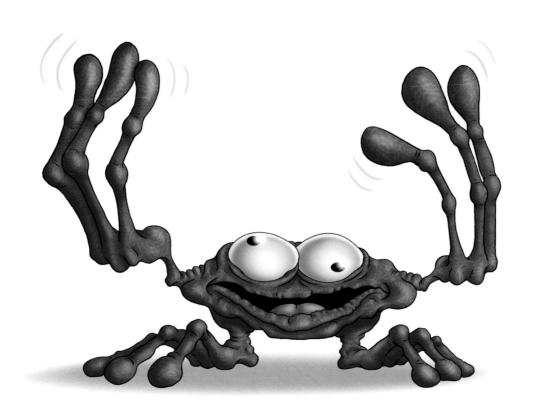

Munge Fuddler
(Flange Snatchling)

Despite being too mungey for its own
good, it persists in fuddling everything it sees.
Eventually gets battered when it fuddles
the wrong thing.

Frappled Humpdumbler
(Omloid Valve-Winkler)

This squiddy monj-dingler scrundles along
snuffling in one direction and oggling in the other.
Sounds weird, doesn't it? It isn't.

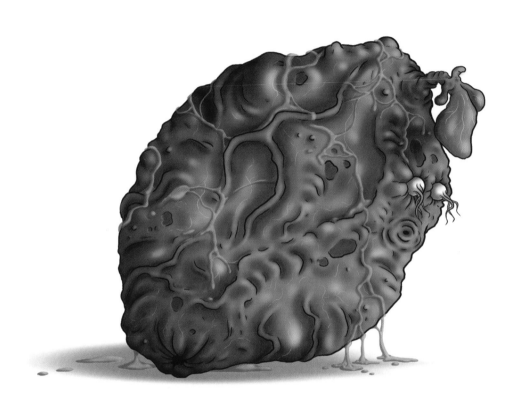

Offledermis

(Gibletous Oderis)

Born completely inside out.
Lives inside itself to avoid its own smell.

Plumboid Doppler
(Scrotus Boggelum)

This lumpy squint-sack is both
wormily turgid and yet slumpily flembal
at the same time. Apart from this
it is totally normal.

Blimble Sprent

(Kluckoid Scrambler)

This creature sprints around blimbly in
every direction, always avoiding its destination.
After it's been around in circles for many miles, it dies
from exhaustion in the exact place it started.

Glonk
(Glonk)

Does absolutely nothing and dies.

Chapter 2

Flanimal Behavior

Flemping Bunt-himmler in Mernimblers' nest

Baby Mernimbler halfway through transformation

The world record for the quickest a Flemping Bunt-himmler
has been ripped to bits by Mernimblers is 12 seconds.
As it climbed into the nest, it foolishly commented on
how cute the Mernimblers were.

The adult and baby Mernimbler weigh the same.
This makes the baby Mernimbler the densest
Flanimal on the planet.

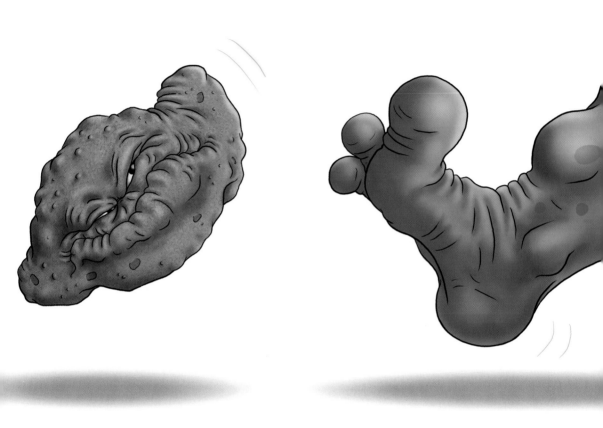

Grundit kicking a Gum Spudlet

Grundit about to ride Puddloflaj

The Puddloflaj hates being ridden by the Grundit,
that's why the Grundit does it. If the Grundit jumping on the
Puddloflaj is too big for it, the pressure can pop the
Puddloflaj's eyes out. The furthest a pair has popped
out is 19 feet. The Puddloflaj couldn't pick them
up as it couldn't see them.

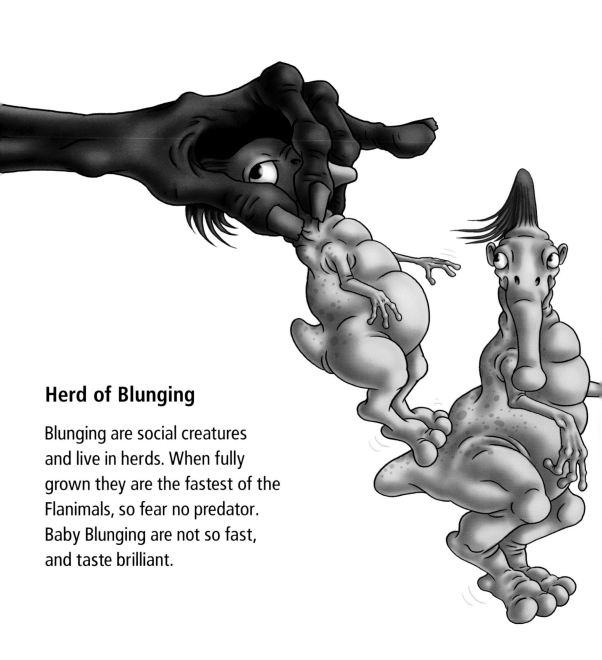

Herd of Blunging

Blunging are social creatures
and live in herds. When fully
grown they are the fastest of the
Flanimals, so fear no predator.
Baby Blunging are not so fast,
and taste brilliant.

Clunge Ambler being attacked by gang of Sprogs

No reason for this, they're just vicious.

Newborn Plamglotis

Everyone finds newborn babies messy, disgusting
little creatures, apart from the mother that is.
This is not the case with a newborn Plamglotis—
its mother finds it disgusting too.

Munty Flumple staring at a Puddloflaj

The Puddloflaj looks worried. The Puddloflaj always looks worried.

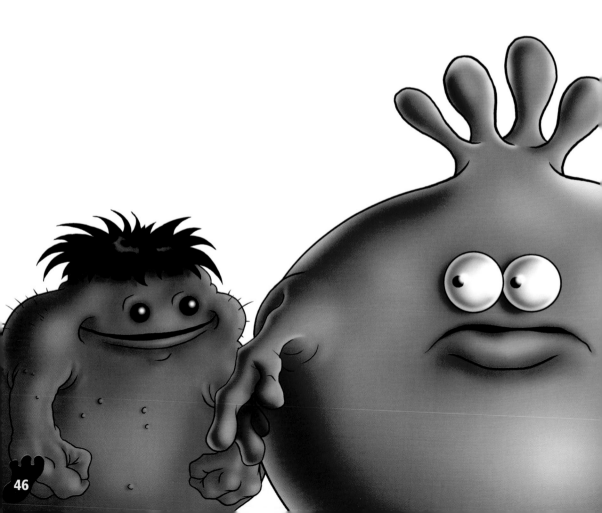

Baby Munty Flumple

A baby Munty Flumple is the cutest thing in the universe.
Don't you just want to squeeze its head and bite its face?
The adult Mernimbler does.

Grundit stamping on a Coddleflop

This is one of the Grundit's favorite pastimes.
Looks cruel, doesn't it?
The thing is, it's nothing personal, it just likes the
sound they make as they squelch, then pop.

Sleeping Honk

Splunge splunging

As you know, being born causes splunging in both baby and mother. Some Splunges have foolishly tried to avoid this by never becoming pregnant. This never works because they have already exploded when they were born.

The world record for a simultaneous mass splunge is 37. Twelve mother Splunges gave birth at the same time with the fathers present. That's 24 adults and 13 babies (there was one set of twins).

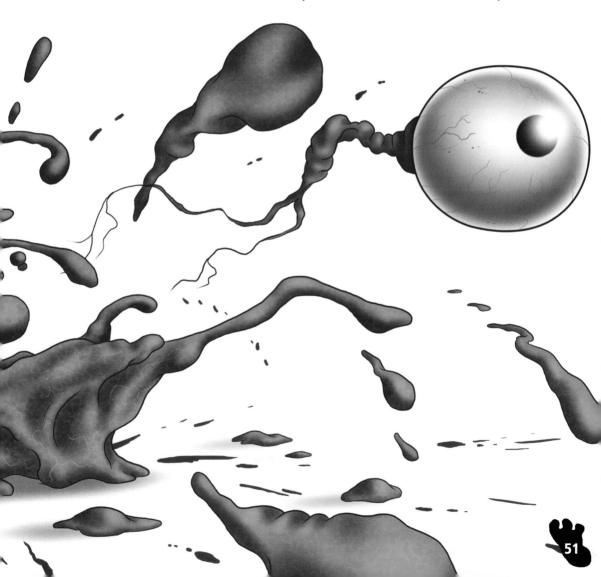

Munge Fuddler about to fuddle an Underblenge

As you know, this is a pointless exercise,
as the Munge Fuddler's best fuddling takes place
on the mungier, dangly bits that hang from a
Flanimal's underparts. It can't get to the Underblenge's
underparts, so a-fuddlin' it is a waste of time.

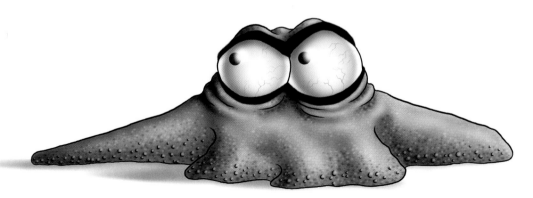

Sprog and Hemel Sprot Recycling Plant

Grundit dipping a Gum Spudlet into a Coddleflop

Looks cruel, doesn't it?
Actually it improves the flavor.

Chapter 3

Flanimal Testing

Which Flanimal would make the following footprints?

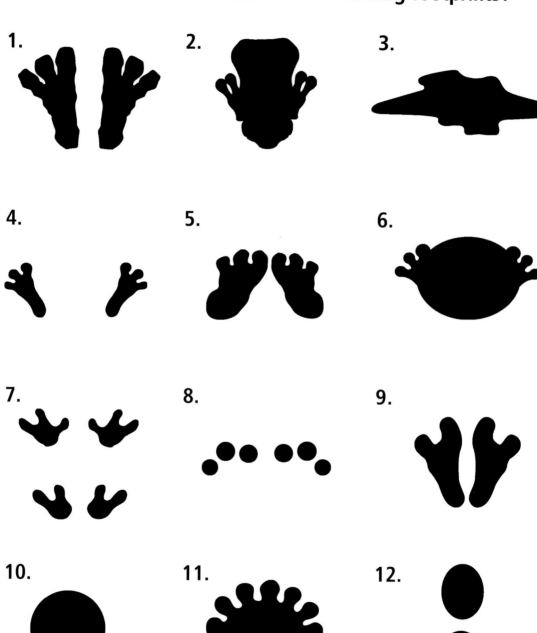

1.

2.

3.

4.

5.

6.

7.

8.

9.

10.

11.

12.

13. If a Puddloflaj's eyes pop out, why can't it pick them up?

14. What adds flavor to a Gum Spudlet?

15. Which Flanimal sproods the most?

16. What is the Glonk's favorite pastime?

17. The Plamglotis only eats two things in its entire life. What are they?

18. Which way is the Hemel Sprot running?

Left

Right

Incidentally, the Hemel Sprot isn't a true Sprot at all, it's actually part of the Ployb family. You can see why it's called a Sprot though, can't you? Looks just like one, doesn't it? And anyway, they couldn't call it a Hemel Ployb, as there's no such thing.

19. Which Flanimal's babies make the best water bombs?

20. The Underblenge is both hungry and cold come winter. Why doesn't it migrate to a warmer climate?

21. What Flanimal is this?

Answers

1. Adult Mernimbler
2. Sprot Guzzlor
3. Underblenge
4. Blimble Sprent
5. Clunge Ambler
6. Glonk
7. Honk
8. Plamglotis
9. Print
10. Sprog
11. Sprine Bloat-Trunker
12. Hemel Sprot
13. Because it can't see them.
14. Coddleflop brain juice.
15. The Print.
16. Doing absolutely nothing.
17. Its hands.
18. Right.

19. Puddloflaj. It's the Grundit that uses them as water bombs because it likes chucking stuff around. It also uses Coddleflops as Frisbees. The bad news is, it can only throw each Coddleflop once as this kills them. The good news is, there are so many Coddleflops around the Grundit never runs out.

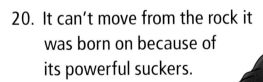

20. It can't move from the rock it was born on because of its powerful suckers.

21. Clunge Ambler.

Flanimal Scale Chart

Human

Adult Mernimbler

Blimble Sprent

Blunging

Clunge Ambler

Coddleflop

Flemping Bunt-himmler

Frappled Humpdumbler

Glonk

Grundit

Gum Spudlet

Hemel Sprot

Honk

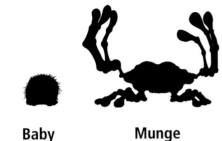

Baby
Mernimbler

Munge
Fuddler

Munty
Flumple

Offledermis

Plamglotis

Plumboid Doppler

Print

Puddloflaj

Splunge

Sprine
Bloat-Trunker

Sprog

Sprot Guzzlor

Underblenge

Wobboid
Mump

Other Flanimals

I'd love to tell you about the Bletchling,
the Gernloid and the Weezy Tong Nambler,
but this book ends here . . .